Gerald Molloy

The Passion play at Ober-Ammergau in the summer of 1871

Gerald Molloy

The Passion play at Ober-Ammergau in the summer of 1871

ISBN/EAN: 9783741194986

Manufactured in Europe, USA, Canada, Australia, Japa

Cover: Foto ©Andreas Hilbeck / pixelio.de

Manufactured and distributed by brebook publishing software
(www.brebook.com)

Gerald Molloy

The Passion play at Ober-Ammergau in the summer of 1871

The Stage and the Chorus.

THE
PASSION PLAY

AT

OBER-AMMERGAU,

IN THE SUMMER OF 1871.

BY THE REV.

GERALD MOLLOY, D.D.,

PROFESSOR OF THEOLOGY IN THE ROYAL COLLEGE OF SAINT PATRICK, MAYNOOTH.

"I will hear that play;
"For never anything can be amiss
"When simpleness and duty tender it."
Midsummer Night's Dream.

SECOND EDITION.

LONDON:
BURNS, OATES, & CO., PORTMAN-ST., PORTMAN-SQUARE.
DUBLIN: M'GLASHAN & GILL, UPPER SACKVILLE-STREET.

1872.

DUBLIN:
PRINTED BY JOHN FALCONER,
53, UPPER SACKVILLE-STREET.

CONTENTS.

——:o:——

PART I. INTRODUCTORY.

PART II. DESCRIPTION OF THE PLAY.

4 *Contents.*

6   *Contents.*

—————:o:—————

LIST OF ILLUSTRATIONS.

—:0:—

LIST OF THE PRINCIPAL PERFORMERS.

------:0:------

Character.	Name.	Age.	Profession.
CHRIST,	JOSEPH MAIR,	27,	Wood-carver.
JUDAS,	GREGOR LECHNER,	51,	Wood-carver.
PETER,	JACOB HETT,	60,	Wood-carver.
JOHN,	JOHANN ZWINK,	20,	House-painter.
PILATE,	TOBIAS FLUNGER,	55,	Teacher of Drawing.
HEROD,	FRANZ PAUL LANG,	56,	Master Potter.
ANNAS,	GREGOR STADLER,	51,	Wood-carver.
CAIPHAS,	JOHANN LANG,	36,	Wood-carver.
BARABBAS,	JOHANN ALLINGER,	57,	Day-labourer.
THE BLESSED VIRGIN,	FRANZISKA FLUNGER,	25,	
MARY MAGDALEN,	JOSEPHA LANG,	27,	
LEADER OF THE CHORUS,	JOHANN DIMMER,	41,	Wood-carver.
CONDUCTOR OF THE ORCHESTRA,	JOSEPH GUTZJELL,	48,	Schoolmaster.

GROUP OF APOSTLES.

JOHN.   PETER.
JUDAS.   PHILIP.

THE PASSION PLAY

AT

OBER-AMMERGAU.

PART I.
INTRODUCTORY.

CHAPTER I.

ORIGIN AND HISTORY OF THE PLAY.

IN a pleasant valley of the Highlands of Bavaria is a picturesque village, situated on the banks of the River Ammer, just where it issues from a deep and narrow gorge. The inhabitants, who are simple and primitive in their ways, depend for their livelihood chiefly on the art of wood carving, to which they are greatly devoted, and in which they have attained a high degree of perfection. This little village, which, from its position, is called Ober-Ammergau, is the last resting place in Germany, and, I may almost say, in Europe, of a kind of religious drama that was common enough in times gone by.

It happened, in the year 1633, that a fearful pestilence swept over the districts of Southern Bavaria. For some weeks the secluded valley of the Ammer was free from its deadly breath. All ingress and egress were rigorously forbidden by the local authorities, and every pass was carefully guarded, to shut out the dreaded contagion. At length, however, a native of the place, who had been working in a neighbouring district, wishing to return to his family, eluded the vigilance of the sentries, entered the valley by a secret path, and unconsciously carried the infection with him. In two days he was a corpse. The contagion spread : and, before the end of three weeks, eighty-four of the villagers, about one-fourth of the whole community, had been laid in their graves.

The terrified survivors, having lost all hope in human aid, met together and bound themselves by a solemn promise to God, if He would stay the plague, to give a representation every ten years of the Passion and Death of Christ. From that moment, as the tradition goes, the pestilence was arrested in its course; and those who were already infected quickly recovered. Faithful to their vow, the grateful villagers gave the first representation in the following year, 1634 ; and, ever since, as each ten years have gone round, the Passion Play has been repeated, with constantly increasing taste and skill, and without any diminution of that reverent religious spirit in which it first began.

But the Passion Play at Ober-Ammergau has not been without its vicissitudes. More than once its very existence was threatened: and for its preservation we are chiefly indebted to the pious zeal of the inhabitants. The history of this matter is well deserving of notice.

There are many reasons why the religious drama of the middle ages should be found ill suited to the condition of modern society. First of all, it is scarcely reverent to expose the most sacred things to the ridicule, or even to the indifferent criticism, of free-thinkers; and we all know there will be many free-thinkers, at the present day, amongst a large audience in a public theatre. Besides, many of these religious plays were mixed up with profane and grotesque associations; and, though they may have been looked upon with reverence in ruder times, they would be more likely now to excite feelings of repugnance and disgust. Again, there is the danger of such representations being turned to account, by ingenious speculators, as a means of making money. And, lastly, there is the temptation to intemperance and riot, which is always present when large, promiscuous crowds of people are assembled together.

Influenced by these, and other such considerations, the Archbishop of Salzburg, in the year 1772, issued a manifesto with a view to the general suppression of religious plays. The civil power lent its aid ; and, during the next ten years, vigorous measures were taken for their extinction in the various towns and villages of Southern Germany. But the people of Ober-Ammergau urged the religious obligation of their vow. They represented, too, that their Play, which had been conducted under the enlightened guidance of the Benedictine monks attached to the neighbouring monastery at Ettal, was free from the abuses that existed elsewhere. Their prayer was heard, and a special exception was made in their favour.

In the year 1810 the Passion Play seemed once again on the point of extinction. The monastery

at Ettal had been unhappily suppressed some
years before; and when the monks were gone,
there seemed to be, no longer, any sufficient gua-
rantee that the religious character of the Play
would be upheld.   A decree was accordingly passed
by the authorities at Munich, forbidding its further
celebration.   The energetic villagers, however,
sent deputies to the capital to plead their cause
before the king; and their Play was spared.
From that time it has been left unmolested; and
it now remains, tolerated rather than encouraged
by the civil and ecclesiastical rulers, a solitary
example of the ancient Christian drama.

In addition to the constant revision which the
Play received, for many generations, from the
hands of the Benedictine monks, it has been
greatly improved and embellished within the present century.   When the monastery at Ettal was
suppressed, one of the monks, Ottmar Weis, who
afterwards became Parish Priest of Jesewang,

where he died in 1843, was for some time allowed to retain his convent cell. By him the design of the Play was recast, and a great part of the text was written anew. About the same time the music which is now in use was composed by Rochus Dedler, the village organist and schoolmaster. Previous to the performance of 1850 the text was again revised by the Parish Priest of Ober-Ammergau, Anton Alois Daisenberger, who had been himself a pupil of Ottmar Weis. This venerable man, after a quarter of a century spent in the active work of his Parish, has retired upon a small stipend. But he still lives amongst his people; and during the preparations of the past year he was always ready to encourage them by his presence, and to assist them with his counsel. Neither the text nor the music has ever been published; and they are known in their integrity only to those engaged in the performance.

As the first representation took place in the

year 1634, it will naturally be asked how the decennial repetition has happened to fall on the year
1871. The answer to this question is easily given,
and is not without interest. About the year 1680
it was deemed expedient that each recurring representation should correspond with the beginning
of each successive decade of the century. To attain
this end the time for the next performance was
anticipated by four years; and thus the year 1680
became as it were, a new starting point, from which
the successive periods, of ten years each, were
thenceforth reckoned. The play was, therefore,
really due in 1870; and, in point of fact, it had
been carefully prepared for that year, and five
representations were given. But suddenly the war
broke out: the call to arms rang through the peace-
ful village; and the players had to leave the stage
for the battle-field.

Some of the principal performers were, by royal
authority, exempted from active service, and re-

served for garrison duty. Joseph Mair, who represented Christ, had an interview with the king, and
obtained special leave to retain his long hair, that
he might be ready to resume his part when the
war should be over. The post assigned to him
was in one of the military depôts at Munich. But
the bulk of the able-bodied villagers had to face
the horrors of actual war. Seventy went out to
fight; and, of these, eight have not returned. Two
are sleeping in the deep trenches of the blood-
stained fields of Sedan; five died in the hospitals
of France; and one has not been heard of, but his
fate is scarcely doubtful.

As soon as the war was over the first thought at
Ober-Ammergau was to continue the series of representations which had been so rudely interrupted.
In each decennial celebration the practice is to give
a performance once a week, for about three months
of the summer; and if, on any occasion, the crowd
should be so great that all cannot find a place in

the theatre, an extra performance is given on the following day. This year, accordingly, the Play was acted for the first time, on June the twenty-fourth; and it was repeated once or twice each week until the close of September.

Those who witnessed it early in the season came away greatly impressed with the religious spirit and artistic skill that marked the performance. The news spread abroad that a Highland village in Bavaria was giving to the world such a living picture of the great drama of Redemption as had never before been seen. The name of Ober-Ammergau became famous in the fashionable assemblies of great capitals; and, crowds of eager tourists and pious pilgrims were soon hurrying over the highways of Europe to see the Passion Play of 1871.

CHAPTER II.

THE PLACE AND THE PEOPLE.

My first impressions of Ober-Ammergau and its people may be of some interest to those who have not been there. I find them thus recorded, in my note book, at the time :—

"This is a wonderful place the day before the Passion Play. Though little better than a mountain hamlet, of, perhaps, a thousand inhabitants, it is suddenly inundated with a crowd of tourists, more than five times that number, who have been pouring in, for two days, from all parts of the world. Englishmen are here, of course, and Americans, in abundance. France is in mourning, and has sent but few representatives. But there are Italians in great numbers, and Russians, and even, it is said, some Jews. The bulk, however, of the visitors are Germans; and of these the greater part seem to have come to the Passion Play as to an act of religious worship. Among the English there are many of great note, and high title; peers and peeresses, and members of Parliament, and dignitaries of the Church.

"Happy are they who, with wise foresight, wrote weeks ago, to Madame Sebastian Veit, or Madame Georg Lang, or to Johann Zwink, or to some one of the other village magnates, to engage rooms, and tickets for the Play. When they arrive, travel-stained and weary, they are met with a cordial smile of welcome, they give their names, and, at once, an attendant is at hand to lead them off to some neighbouring house, where rooms have been neatly set in order, and religiously guarded for them. Those who come late, and have made no provision, must be content to wander about by day, and, at night, to lie in the hall or on the staircase, of some hospitable dwelling, after the more fortunate lodgers have gone to bed.

"I had not written before; but I arrived at mid-day on Saturday, and the Play was not to come off until Monday. So, being early in the field, I set to work at once, and, after some hunting about, got shelter and a welcome in the house of an humble family. Speaking comparatively, I may say that I am luxuriously lodged. I have four clean, whitewashed walls all to myself; a bed, a chair, a dressing table; and a second table for writing at, which has been generously supplied by my hostess, not, I fear, without some sacrifice of her personal convenience. The room is lighted by two rustic windows. Over the bed is a crucifix, with the inscription 'Praised be Jesus Christ.' My portmanteau rests on a large and venerable stove. And, when every thing is tidily stowed away, I have just room to move about without coming into collision with my furniture.

"After taking possession of my lodgings, I went

out for half an hour to see the town; and on my return, I found my table adorned with a bunch of wild roses in an earthenware mug. A lovely boy of three years old, and a pretty little girl of eight, were playing about in their bare feet. They were the children of my hostess, and are both to appear in the Play. We soon made friends, and, ever since, they have been my constant and most welcome visitors.

"This was Sunday morning. The Masses began at three o'clock in the Parish Church, and went on without intermission until ten. The Parish Mass, called the *Hoch Amt*, was at half-past eight. It was a Missa Cantata, with Organ, Orchestra, and Choir. The music was simply magnificent. I cannot say if it would entirely satisfy the critical taste of musical scholars. But it seemed to me to rise above the domain of criticism. It burst forth from the lofty organ gallery like a song of joy and triumph coming from a higher and purer sphere. It swelled through the ample nave; it found its way into every heart; and few, I think, who heard it, were disposed to weigh its merits according to the nice laws of musical science.

"Then the devotion of the people was something beautiful to see. Men, women, and children, all had their prayer-books and their beads. Except for a few minutes, they knelt during the whole time of Mass, and were evidently absorbed in earnest, thoughtful prayer. It could not be that a people who had produced such music, in a secluded valley, were insensible to its influence. But they did not come to hear it as a fine display of art. It seemed rather to enter into their souls, and to blend with their prayers, as they knelt before the altar of God. Never before had I witnessed such a combination of refined art with simple, earnest devotion.

"After the Gospel, the music was hushed for a

time, and one of the priests gave a short practical
sermon. The people, apparently out of respect,
stood until he had finished the exordium of his
discourse, and then sat down. When the sermon
was ended the whole congregation joined in
prayer aloud. It was a sort of recitative. The
rich baritone of the men alternated with the con-
tralto of the women; all the voices on each side
being pitched in the same tone, and keeping perfect time. Mass was then resumed, and the
organ again pealed forth. That such a service
should have been given in a village Church, and
by the village people themselves, is certainly wonderful; and it is not less admirable that, in the
presence of so many strangers, it should have
been performed with an entire absence of ostenta-
tion and display.

"Many English Protestants were there, and a
large sprinkling of regular English tourists, a
class not generally remarkable for good behaviour

in Catholic Churches abroad. But here they seemed all deeply impressed with the religious character of the scene. They retired, for the most part, to the rere of the Church, and looked on with attention and respect. What the Play may be to-morrow it is hard to anticipate; but, from what I have seen to-day, I cannot doubt that it will be solemn and impressive."

CHAPTER III.

THE THEATRE.

AT daybreak on Monday, the fourteenth of August, every one was up and stirring in the village of Ober-Ammergau. Though it was not a festival of the Church, Masses were celebrated from a very early hour; for the good people of Bavaria think it a duty to prepare themselves for the spectacle of the day by prayer and Holy Communion. Indeed, if one were to see only what went on within the walls of the Church, he would easily suppose that the crowd which, for two days, had been flocking into this mountain hamlet, were come on a pilgrimage to worship at the Altar of God, and to say their beads before the colossal statue of our Lady.

The *Hoch Amt,* or Parish Mass, began at half-past five. When it was over, the band went playing through the village. This was the signal for the theatre to open: and a long stream of people, eager and enthusiastic, but singularly well conducted, poured down the winding street into the green meadow beyond, where, close to the clear waters of the Ammer, stood a clumsy looking wooden structure of gigantic size. At half-past six the doors were thrown open, and at seven the theatre was full; excepting that part where the seats were numbered and reserved. All the tickets for these seats had been secured a fortnight before; and they who had the good fortune to

possess them would be time enough in another
hour, for the Play was not to begin until eight.
Not being among the fortunate few, I went early
with the crowd; and was rather pleased than
otherwise at having a little time to look about me,
and to glance over a programme of the Play, which
I had picked up on my journey to Ammergau.

The theatre, though plain and simple in its
construction, is admirably adapted to the purpose
for which it is intended. Between two rows of
poplars, in the open meadow, a large space is
enclosed by common timber planking. It is in
shape an oblong rectangle. At one end is erected
a stage of ample dimensions, 120 feet in breadth,
170 in depth. The rest of the enclosure is occu-
pied by the spectators. Plain deal benches are
laid straight across, which rise, one above another,
from the stage to the extreme rere, and afford
accommodation to about 5,000 people. The fore-
most part of the stage, to a depth of about fifty

feet, has no scenery or decoration of any kind. It is here that the chief part of the action takes place. The back is divided into three compartments. That in the centre, which is much the largest, is itself a complete stage of the ordinary kind, with a drop-scene in front, and scenery that changes according to the occasion. To the right of this central compartment, or inner stage, as it may be called, is the house of Annas, to the left, the house of Pilate; each with a balcony in front. These balconies, as will appear in the sequel, have a prominent part in the performance. Beyond the houses, on either hand, are the side compartments. They are provided with fixed scenery, which represents the streets of Jerusalem stretching away in the distance; and are much used for the various processions introduced throughout the Play. The theatre is open to the sky, except the inner stage, and about one-third of the benches, which are protected by a thin covering of boards.

From every part of the theatre there is a good view of the stage. But, for the convenience of visitors, it has been railed off into various divisions. The scale of charges for admission is exceedingly low, ranging from ten pence to about five shillings: for the high-minded villagers have no thought of making money of their play. Out of the proceeds a small sum is paid to the principal performers; which is, however, scarcely sufficient to compensate them for the time expended in preparing their parts. Whatever surplus remains at the end of the season, after all expenses have been defrayed, is devoted to works of charity, or of public utility.

And here I cannot help observing that the same praiseworthy spirit prevails throughout every department of business in this primitive village. There is no disposition to extort money, notwithstanding the temptation offered by the enormous influx of visitors. At the inns and private

houses the charges for accommodation are singularly moderate : and the beautiful carvings in
wood, which have been wrought, in the long
winter nights, with infinite labour and surprising
skill, are sold at prices that but ill repay the
artists.

It was a curious sight that vast audience of
5,000 people, as they sat waiting, in eager expec-
tation, for the Play to begin. Artists and critics,
poets, historians and philosophers, statesmen and
soldiers, church dignitaries and men of science,
people of noble rank and people of boundless
wealth, were gathered together from the ends of
the world, to witness the Drama of Redemption
represented by the untravelled peasants of a
mountain village. Yet these were but a handful,
compared to the more humble pilgrims who had
come from the neighbouring districts of Bavaria
and the Tyrol, and from the various towns of
Catholic Germany. Great numbers appeared in

the peculiar costumes of their respective countries, which, by their bright colours and picturesque character, added not a little to the liveliness and variety of the scene. Perfect good humour prevailed; but there was no levity of manner: and any attempt to turn the Play into ridicule was sure to meet with instant and effective reproof.

Beyond this crowded mass of human beings, and beyond the wooden walls that bounded the enclosure where we sat, the green meadows of the valley were distinctly visible, shut in by a glorious amphitheatre of hills. At first the hills and the valley were bathed in mist; and the pretty village of Unter-Ammergau, two miles away, was scarcely discernible as it lay sleeping in the gray light of morning. But, little by little, the mist cleared off, and the sun began to creep down the slopes of the mountain, giving to the corn fields a more golden hue, and to the meadows a brighter green. The trees, waving in the wind, cast their

long shadows down the valley towards the west;
the cattle grazed lazily over the rich pastures; while
at intervals, as if to heighten by contrast the
beauty of the scene, large patches of cloud dark-
ened, for a moment, the landscape, as they flitted
across the sky. It will be easily believed that a
scene like this, together with the pure fresh breeze
of the mountains, lent a very peculiar and picturesque charm to the rustic theatre of Ober-
Ammergau.

CHAPTER IV.

SCOPE AND DESIGN OF THE PLAY.

THE design of the Play is to present, in living
reality, a striking picture of our Lord's Passion,
beginning with His triumphal entry into Jerusalem on the Sunday before He suffered, and ending with His Resurrection and final Ascension

SIMON.

LAZARUS. MARTHA.

into Heaven. All the events of the Gospel narrative are portrayed with perfect fidelity : but the Gospel narrative is expanded, and, so to speak, interpreted, by means of dialogue and dramatic action. This was, no doubt, a difficult and delicate task to undertake; but it has been accomplished with judgment and skill. The several narratives of the four Evangelists have been blended together into one complete history; the apparent contradictions or inconsistencies, with which every one is familiar who has made a special study of the Passion, have been admirably adjusted; and, in the dramatic additions which have been made, every word, every movement, is in beautiful harmony with the tone and spirit of the Sacred Text.

With a view to make the representation more impressive, and to bring out the intimate connexion between the Old Covenant and the New, the successive events in Our Lord's Passion are preceded by one or more types from the history of the Old Testament. These types are, perhaps, to an ordinary spectator, the greatest charm of the Play. They are represented on the inner stage by *Tableaux Vivants*, which display an artistic taste, and a skill for effective grouping, not unworthy of the most cultivated city in Europe, and certainly wonderful to discover among the peasantry of a mountain village.

There is a third element in the Passion Play which contributes not a little to its dramatic effect. At stated intervals, on the front stage, appears a bright-robed train of choristers, whose part it is to explain, sometimes by monologue, but generally by song, the Tableau which is disclosed to view at the same moment, and to interpret its typical signification. They suggest appropriate sentiments, and express, in beautiful and touching poetry, the anxieties, fears, and hopes which may be supposed to fill the breast of a spectator. Sometimes they pray to God to deliver Christ from the hands of His enemies; sometimes they expostulate with the Jews; sometimes they call upon the audience to walk in the footsteps of the suffering Redeemer.

It will be observed that the function assigned to this band of singers is almost exactly the same as that which belonged to the Chorus in the classical plays of ancient Greece. And yet, curiously enough, there is reason to believe that this feature in the Passion Play is not the result of any conscious imitation, but has been developed rather, in the course of time, by the exigencies of the performance, and the dramatic taste of the Highland peasantry. The German text of the choral odes has been published, and occasional specimens will be given in the following pages, from which some idea may be formed of their general character and spirit.

PART II.

DESCRIPTION OF THE PLAY.

PROLOGUE,

ILLUSTRATED WITH TWO TABLEAUX.

EXACTLY at eight o'clock the boom of a cannon was heard, and the music of the Orchestra began. At first it was faint and low; but the vast audience was hushed into perfect stillness, and every note was distinctly heard. Gradually the music swelled in volume and power; and, as the first great bursts of harmony sent a

thrill through every frame, the choristers entered
from either side of the front stage, clad in white
embroidered tunics, over which were gracefully
flung brilliant mantles of scarlet, green, or blue.
They moved across the stage with a singular grace
and majesty of deportment, and formed in a line
facing the audience. The leader was in the centre,
and the others were ranged at either side, according
to height, the lowest being placed at the extremities
of the line.

It was a lovely picture as they stood there in
the morning sun, with their long flowing hair,
and their brilliant robes, and their sandalled feet.
Accompanied by the Orchestra they proclaim in
song the great Drama about to be represented.
The human race, bowed down under the curse of
God, is doomed to death. But mercy comes from
Sion. The Eternal is not always angry with His
people. He will redeem them in the blood of His
only Son.

TABLEAU I. ADAM AND EVE EXPELLED FROM THE GARDEN OF EDEN.—*Gen.* iii. 23, 24. As they sing of

> "Man's first disobedience, and the fruit
> Of that forbidden tree whose mortal taste
> Brought death into the world,"

the curtain of the inner stage slowly rises behind. The Choristers, dividing in the middle, fall back, right and left, so as to form a line on either side, stretching outwards from the extremities of the drop-scene towards the front of the stage, and the first Tableau is disclosed to view. It is the Garden of Eden, with the Tree of Life in the middle, and, at a little distance, the Tree of the Knowledge of Good and Evil. Flowers and fruits are blooming around, and all looks fair and pleasant. But an Angel stands in front, and guards the entrance, with his bright sword lifted aloft and gleaming in the sun. Adam and Eve are seen on the right, in the act of retiring. They glance at the Angel, and seem to start back with a look of awe and shame. After a few minutes, during which the figures remain motionless as statues, the drop-scene falls ; the Choristers form again into a single line, and announce the coming of a Redeemer.

TABLEAU II. THE SYMBOL OF REDEMPTION.—As the curtain rises on the second Tableau the Choristers again divide and fall back as before. A large cross is seen erect in the background. Around it are grouped a number of children on their knees, and an Angel points to it as the Symbol of Redemption. The Choristers, too, fall upon their knees, and a plaintive chant is sung, which admirably expresses the moral of the Play.

These two pictures,—Man fallen by Sin, and redeemed by the Cross,—together with the chant of the Chorus which reaches the hearts of all, constitute a beautiful introduction to the drama of the Passion. The effect is immediate and universal. Every one is impressed with the solemnity, the religious spirit, the good taste, that mark the performance. Prejudice, if it existed, is disarmed; the apprehension of irreverence or profanation is dispelled. When the chant is ended the Choristers withdraw behind the scenes on either side, and the First Act of the Passion Play begins.

_____

ACT I.

TRIUMPHAL ENTRY INTO JERUSALEM.

Joyful shouts are heard in the distance: presently, winding down the streets of Jerusalem, a motley crowd is seen of men and women, youths

and maidens, and little children. They are clad
in oriental dresses; they carry green branches in
their hands, and cry out, as they move along,
" Hosannah to the Son of David." In the midst
of the throng is a striking figure, seated on an
ass, and clothed in a long flowing purple robe,
with a crimson cloak. This is Joseph Mair, who
represents the Christ. He is about six feet in
height, of graceful form, and calm dignified deportment. His features have an olive tint, and
convey the idea of serious thought and patient
endurance. In his manner there is a wonderful
combination of majesty with gentleness and simplicity. His jet black hair is parted down the
middle and falls loosely over his shoulders.
Around him are grouped the twelve Apostles,
dressed in similar robes, but of plainer material
and more gaudy colours. Each carries a staff in
his hand: and already, in their looks and bearing, one may detect the traces of those various

CHRIST IN THE TEMPLE.   CHRIST AT THE LAST SUPPER.
THE LEADER OF THE CHORUS.   ANNAS, THE HIGH PRIEST.

characteristics which are developed as the Play proceeds.

Meanwhile the Chief Priests and Scribes approach from the opposite side of the stage, and confront the Christ. They question him with haughty arrogance, and hear, with ill-disguised rage and jealousy, the shouts and applause of the people. At this time there could not have been less than two hundred people on the stage; and all, even to the little children led by the hand, performed their parts with simple good taste, without any apparent effort, or any straining after theatrical effect.

While all eyes are fixed on the great Central Figure, for the first time brought face to face with his enemies, the curtain of the inner stage is uplifted, and before us is the Temple, where money-changers are driving bargains, and dealers are buying and selling. Christ enters amongst them, with great dignity, as one who has power.

He overturns the tables of the money-changers, and, making a scourge of small cords, he drives out of the temple those who were buying and selling, using the words of Scripture: "It is written, 'My house is a house of prayer;' but you have made it a den of thieves."

An uproar ensues. The Pharisees, urged on by wounded pride, and the money-changers by avarice, make common cause together. They charge Christ with rebellion against the law of Moses and the Prophets. The Chief Priests try to excite a rising among the people, and cry out: "With us, all that belong to Moses! Moses is our Prophet! Revenge! Revenge!" Mildly, but with an air of authority, Christ rebukes their hypocrisy; and then, taking leave of the crowd, turns away in the direction of Bethania.

ACT II.

THE HIGH COURT OF THE JEWS IN COUNCIL.

TABLEAU. THE BRETHREN OF JOSEPH CONSPIRE AGAINST HIM.—*Gen.* xxxvii. 18–24. The Choristers, entering as before, introduce by song the story of Joseph. They tell how his brothers, instigated by jealousy, conspired together for his destruction; and then they explain how the Scribes and Pharisees were driven by the same evil passion to conspire against our Lord. Meanwhile the curtain of the inner stage rises; they fall back in two lines, right and left; and the Tableau appears. It is the wilderness of Dothain. The pit is there into which Joseph has been thrown. Two of his brothers are looking into it: the rest are standing about in groups. All is motionless, and the Chorus explains the significance of the type.

As the Chorus retires the curtain of the inner stage is drawn up, and before us, sitting in council, is the Sanhedrim, the great High Court of the Jews. Annas, with snow-white beard, and Caiphas, a much younger and more vigorous-looking man, of commanding aspect, occupy the principal seats in the centre of the background.

The Chief Priests and the Pharisees are ranged around, on elevated benches, and the Scribes are seated at desks, in the middle of the hall. They make a brilliant show with their varied and gorgeous costumes, which, in shape and character, are designed, as far as may be, according to the evidence of Scripture illustrated by archæological research.

The debate begins; and it soon becomes evident that their hearts are filled with pride and envy. "The whole world runs after him," they say. But they know how to cloak their evil passions under a mantle of virtue. It is not their pride that is hurt, no; it is religion and the people that are in danger. "The Romans will come and take away our place and nation." Many speeches are made, but they all tend in the same direction; and the words of the High Priest are echoed from every bench, "It is better one man should die and that the whole nation perish not."

It only remains to discover some means by which they may get possession of Christ, without exciting a tumult among the people. They call in the aid of the money-changers, whose counters were overturned by our Lord in the Temple. One of these men is acquainted with Judas. He eagerly enters into the wicked designs of the Court: he engages to test the fidelity of Judas, and, by promises of gold, to induce him to deliver up his Master. With this the debate is closed, and the curtain falls.

ACT III.

CHRIST IN BETHANIA BEFORE HIS PASSION.

TABLEAU I. YOUNG TOBIAS TAKING LEAVE OF HIS PARENTS.— *Tob.* v. 20–28. This Tableau and the one that follows are intended to typify the parting of Christ from His Blessed Mother and His friends in Bethania, when the hour of His Passion had arrived. The young Tobias appears in the freshness of youth, with a sorrowful and dejected countenance. One hand he gives to the Archangel Raphael, who stands by his side; the other is held in the

grasp of his weeping mother. Behind, stands the old
blind father, in the act of giving his parting benediction.
Close to this group, on the right, is the paternal dwelling;
and, at a little distance, on the left, is seen the faithful
maid servant in tears. The Chorus, explaining the significance of the Tableau, sings of the mother's sorrow in a
sweet and tender melody.

> " Freunde, welch ein herber Schmerz
> Folterte das Mutterherz,
> Als Tobias, an der Hand
> Raphaels, in fremdes Land
> Auf Befehl des Vaters eilte."

> " Friends, what a bitter grief oppressed
> That loving mother's breast,
> When, with Raphael, hand in hand,
> Tobias to a stranger land
> Went at his father's best."

TABLEAU II. THE FORLORN BRIDE LAMENTS THE ABSENCE
OF HER BELOVED.—*Cant.* v. 8–17. The scene is a garden
in fairest bloom. The bride is there in her bridal robes.
Around her are grouped the daughters of Jerusalem,
arrayed in white, with girdles of blue, and adorned with
wreaths of flowers. In the midst of all this show of
joyousness the Bride is sad and disconsolate. She looks
to the maidens for comfort, and they return her look
with glances of sympathy. All the figures remain fixed
as. marble statues while the choral ode is sung.

THE YOUNG TOBIAS TAKING LEAVE OF HIS PARENTS.

" Wo is er hin? Wo ist er hin,
    Der Schöne aller Schönen?
Mein Auge weinet, ach! um ihn
    Der Liebe heisse Thränen.

" Ach komme doch! ach, komme doch,
    Sieh diese Thränen fliessen:
Geliebter, wie? Du zögerst noch
    Dich an mein Herz zu schliessen?

" Mein Auge forschet überall
    Nach Dir auf allen Wegen;
Und mit der Sonne erstem Strahl
    Eilt Dir mein Herz entgegen."

" Where is my love departed,
    The fairest of the fair?
Mine eyes gush out with burning tears
    Of love, and grief, and care.

" Ah! come again! ah! come again!
    To this deserted breast.
Beloved one! oh! why tarriest thou
    Upon my heart to rest?

" By every path, on every way,
    Mine eyes are strained to greet thee;
And with the earliest beam of day
    My heart leaps forth to meet thee."*

---

* For this translation, and for some of those that follow, I am indebted to an interesting article on the Passion Play, which appeared in Macmillan's Magazine, October, 1860.

The Chorus retires, and Christ appears, with his twelve Apostles, in the village of Bethania, discoursing with them on his approaching Passion. He is met by Simon, who invites him to come and sup at his house. The invitation is graciously accepted, and they all withdraw together. A moment after, the curtain of the inner stage rises, and we are shown a great hall in the house of Simon. The supper table is laid. Our Lord enters with his Apostles, and they take their seats. Martha waits upon the guests: while Mary Magdalen, bearing in her hand a box of precious ointment, softly enters the hall, and glances hastily around. As soon as her eyes fall on the figure of Christ she throws herself prostrate before him, and then rising pours the ointment over his head. Afterwards, breaking the box, she anoints his feet, and wipes them lovingly with her long and flowing hair.

Judas complains of the waste with an earnestness that half reveals his secret lust of money.

He argues, with an air of piety, that the ointment might have been sold for more than three hundred pence, and given to the poor. Some of the other Apostles, too, though with greater composure of manner, condemn the waste, and murmur against Mary Magdalen. Then follows the gentle rebuke of Christ, in the words of Scripture, "Why trouble ye this woman? She hath wrought a good work upon me. For the poor you have always with you, but me you have not always. Amen I say to you, wheresoever this Gospel shall be preached in the whole world, that also which she hath done shall be told for a memory of her."

Going forth from the supper room, Christ meets his mother, who has come, attended by some faithful friends, to bid him a last farewell. The overwhelming grief of the mother, the tenderness and dignity of the son, were portrayed in this scene with taste and feeling. Nevertheless I could not help thinking that the performance was here, for the first time, inadequate to the occasion. Indeed the task was too much for human powers: and it is scarcely a censure to say that Franzisca Flunger, who acted the part of our Blessed Lady, failed to express fully that singular combination of love, and grief, and reverence, which must have filled the heart of Mary when she stretched out her arms to embrace, for the last time, Him who was at once her Son and her God.

ACT IV.

CHRIST'S LAST JOURNEY TO JERUSALEM.

TABLEAU. QUEEN VASTHI REJECTED BY ASSUERUS; ESTHER CHOSEN IN HER STEAD.—*Esther*, i. ii. This Tableau, which symbolizes the rejection of the Jews and the call of the Gentiles, is chiefly rendered effective by the beautiful chant of the Chorus. When the curtain rises, King Assuerus, seated on his throne, and surrounded by his courtiers, is seen in the act of choosing for his Queen the humble Esther, instead of Vasthi, whom he spurns for disobedience. Singularly touching, indeed, are the plaintive strains to which the following words are sung:—

THE BLESSING.

THE CHRIST.

JOHN.   PETER.

" Jerusalem ! Jerusalem !
Bekehre dich zu deinem Gott !
Verachte nicht mit Frevelspott
  Den Mahnungsruf der Gnade ;
Dass nicht, Unsel'ge, über dich
Dereinst in vollen Schalen sich
  Des Höchsten Grimm entlade ! "

" Jerusalem ! Jerusalem !
Turn thee unto thy God ; oh, turn !
Do not, with wicked mockery, spurn
  The warning call of grace ;
That not, in fullest measure, be
The wrath of God outpoured on thee,
  And all thy hapless race."

The Choristers retire, and Christ is seen approaching with his Apostles, on his last journey to Jerusalem. When he comes in sight of the unhappy city, he laments over it, and bewails its future desolation. Peter and John get instructions to go before and prepare the Passover. They set forth at once, having first, on their knees, received their Master's blessing. As the Saviour touches on the subject of his impending Passion,

Judas impudently breaks in: "Prithee, Master, wilt thou not make some provision for our future wants? How useful now were those three hundred pence!" The other Apostles look at him with an expression of surprise and indignation: but the Saviour meekly says, "Dear friend, put thy trust in my words." Then Judas rejoins, with uprising anger, "Am I not the purse-bearer, and who will take care of us if I do not?" Jesus only answers with gentle words of warning.

Meanwhile they approach the city: but Judas lags behind. His fingers clutch the almost empty money-bag that hangs from his girdle; and he murmurs at his hard service and scanty reward. Avarice and discontent are gnawing at his heart. While he is dallying with his thoughts, the money-changers, sent by the Chief Priests, come to tempt him. First one, then another, appears upon the scene. For a time he is undecided. A conflict of good and evil is going on within him.

Money, which has long been the chief joy and treasure of his soul, allures him on. " Ah, the three hundred pence!" he says; "now is the time to make good my loss. The money is already within my grasp. I must not let it slip from my fingers." Then again, some lingering feelings of affection and gratitude stir within his heart, and he shrinks from the deed of treachery to which his evil counsellors would hurry him. Musing with himself, he says: " But the Master is a good man; and I, who have been so often a witness of his goodness, and a sharer in it too, how can I be so base as to betray him!"

His mind, thus tossed about by conflicting emotions, is troubled and restless. One moment he listens to the insidious promises of the tempters; the next, he seems to drive them away. He resolves, and he changes his mind. In the end he becomes desperate; he gives his word, appoints a time to appear before the Sanhedrim, and then hurries after his Divine Master to the supper room.

This scene is admirable in every way; in the conception of the author, as well as in the performance of the actor. It traces very intelligibly the headlong fall of Judas; and presents a fearful picture of the power which passion exercises when it once becomes dominant in the soul.

ACT V.

THE LAST SUPPER.

TABLEAU I. THE MANNA IN THE DESERT.—*Exod.* xvi. 4–15. The people of Israel are seen gathered together in the wilderness of Sin. Manna is coming down upon them from Heaven, and they are looking up in wonder and thankfulness. Men, women, and children, to the number of about three hundred, clad in every variety of costume appropriate to their condition in life, take part in this living picture; which is not less remarkable for the perfect stillness of each individual figure than for the artistic effect of the whole group. While the spectators gaze upon the scene with admiration a choral ode explains the type, and reminds the audience that, whereas they who ate of the Manna in the desert are dead, they who eat of the Living Bread in the New Covenant shall live for ever.

Tableau II. The Great Bunch of Grapes carried home from the Land of Chanaan.—*Numb.* xiii. 24. The inner stage is again crowded with the people of Israel; while, through their midst, a monster bunch of grapes is borne, on a lever, by two of the spies from the Land of Chanaan; a beautiful figure of the Eucharist which, in like manner, comes to weary wanderers in the desert of life, as an earnest of the far-off Promised Land.

The reality quickly follows on the type. Peter and John, who were sent forward to make ready the Passover, appear in the streets of Jerusalem. They meet the man " carrying a pitcher of water." They accost him; and he takes them to his Master. The supper room is already laid out; and, in a few minutes, Christ arrives with the rest of the party. When he meets the goodman of the house he gives him his blessing, " Peace be with thee and with thy whole house." He then sits down to table with his twelve Apostles.

The scene that follows exhibits, perhaps, more

than other in the Play, the deep Scriptural learn-
ing, and the rare artistic taste, which seem to
have found a home in the valley of Ammergau.
Not to speak of the dramatic difficulties that
surround such a subject, every one knows that the
mere arrangement of the incidents which cluster
round the Last Supper has been a puzzle to Com-
mentators from the beginning. It was necessary
to make a choice between a great variety of
conflicting opinions: and the choice which has
been made shows good judgment, and a minute
knowledge of the Sacred Text. First comes the
Paschal meal : towards the close of it, a strife arises
among the Apostles which of them should be
accounted the greatest : then follows the Washing
of the Feet, in which our Lord gives a signal
example of humility : next, the Institution of
the Eucharist : afterwards, the announcement
is made that "one of you will betray me," but
so, that the Apostles remain uncertain which of

them it is : lastly, the sop is given, and Judas goes out.

Nothing could be more admirable than the air of majesty and solemn reverence with which the chief part in all these incidents was enacted by Joseph Mair. When he took the bread in his hands, and, rising from the table, lifted up his eyes to Heaven, and pronounced those sacred words so familiar to all Christians, the audience was hushed into breathless silence. He distributed the Eucharist to the twelve, beginning on his right hand, and going round to each in succession, until he came back again to his own place. The Apostles, though they remained sitting, received it with extraordinary reverence : and, when the Christ had passed by, each of them was seen with his head bowed down and his hands clasped in prayer. Judas alone was an exception, who took his part in the ceremony with a cold formality and a look of conscious guilt.

Soon after the distribution of the Eucharist follow the words of Christ, "Amen, I say to you, that one of you is about to betray me." Grief and alarm are depicted on every face. One after another, they ask, stretching over the table, " Is it I, Lord?" He answers, "One of the twelve, one who dippeth his hand with me in the dish." Even Judas tries to assume an air of concern, and asks, though not with the same earnestness as the rest, "Master, is it I?" The answer is given to himself, and is not perceived by the other Apostles, at least not by all of them, "Thou hast said it." Then John, leaning on the bosom of Christ, asks, at the suggestion of Peter, " Who is it, Lord?" He receives, but only for himself, the answer, " It is he to whom I shall give the morsel of bread when I have dipped it." And the morsel is given to Judas with the words, " What thou dost, do quickly." Judas receives it, and hastens out of the room, with a desperate

THE LAST SUPPER.

resolve depicted on his countenance to finish the deed of evil he has begun.

The Apostles, still uncertain who the traitor is, are startled by the sudden departure of Judas, and their suspicions are. aroused. Thomas at once asks, "Where is Judas gone?" Various suggestions are made, but the subject is not pursued; for Christ takes up the discourse with the words, "My little children, yet a little while I am with you. You shall seek me, and, as I said to the Jews, 'Whether I go you cannot come,' so I say to you now. A new commandment I give unto you, that you love one another as I have loved you. By this shall all men know that you are my disciples, that you have love one for another." Then Peter cries out with great earnestness. "Lord, whither goest thou?" The Saviour answers, "Whither I go thou canst not follow me now, but thou shalt follow hereafter." Hereupon Peter protests, "Why cannot I follow thee now?

I will lay down my life for thee." But Christ replies, with a look of admonition, "Thou wilt lay down thy life for me! Amen, amen, I say to thee, before the cock shall crow thou wilt deny me thrice." After these words they say a prayer in common, and all go out together on the way to Gethsemani.

ACT VI.

TREACHERY OF JUDAS.

TABLEAU. JOSEPH SOLD BY HIS BRETHREN.—*Gen.* xxxvii. 25–31. The wilderness of Dothain is again before us. Joseph has been drawn out of the pit, and is standing in the background, imploring for mercy by his looks. But he implores in vain: he has been sold by his brothers for twenty pieces of silver;—a fitting type of the Saviour of the world sold for money by his chosen disciple. The Ismaelite merchants are seen in the act of paying down the price of blood. On one side are their camels laden with merchandise; on the other, some of Joseph's brothers are staining his many-coloured coat in the blood of a kid. The chant of the Chorus is simple and touching.

"'Was bietet für den Knaben ihr?'
So sprechen Brüder, 'wenn euch wir
   Ihn käuflich übergeben?'
Sie geben bald um den Gewinn
Von zwanzig Silberlingen hin
   Des Bruders Blut und Leben.

"'Was gebet ihr?—wie lohnt ihr mich?'
Spricht der Iskariot, 'wenn ich
   Den Meister euch verrathe?'
Um dreissig Silberlinge schliesst
Den Blutbund er, und Jesus ist
   Verkauft dem hohen Rathe.

"Was hier sich uns vor Augen stellt
Ist ein getreues Bild der Welt:
   Wie oft habt ihr, durch eure Thaten,
   Auch euren Gott verkauft, verrathen!"

"'What will you give us for the lad,'
So Joseph's wicked brethren said,
   'Him at our hands receiving?'
Soon on the sum they are agreed,
For twenty silver pieces' meed
   Their brother's life-blood giving.

"'What will you give for my reward,'
Iscariot saith, 'if I my Lord
   Betray to you for gold?'

The bond, the bond of blood, is signed,
And Christ is to his foes consigned,
  His precious Life-blood sold.

"A scene of woe; yet much I fear,
A picture of the world is here;
How oft have ye in deeds denied him,
How oft betrayed and crucified Him!"*

When the music has ceased the curtain rises,
and we find ourselves again in the presence of the
High Court of the Sanhedrim, with the Chief
Priests and the Pharisees- assembled in Council.
Judas is brought before them. After some debate
a bargain is agreed to; and he engages to deliver
Christ into their hands for thirty pieces of silver.
Joseph of Arimathea and Nicodemus raise their
voices against this iniquitous proceeding. But
they only bring down upon themselves the angry
maledictions of Caiphas: and, finding that their
protest is of no avail, they leave the Court.

In the meantime the money is brought in by

---

* See the Monthly Packet, July, 1871.

The Sanhedrim in Council:
Judas Receives the Thirty Pieces of Silver.

one of the Scribes, and counted out to Judas. Nervously he clutches each coin as it drops on the table; and counts the whole over again, with an eagerness that forcibly portrays the absorbing passion of his soul. A time and place are appointed for the deed of treachery, and the wretched man, buckling on his money-bag to his girdle, hurries away from the scene of his guilty compact. The Pharisees, however, too wise in the wisdom of the world to trust a traitor's word, appoint one of their number to keep him in sight. Congratulations are now exchanged between the members of the Council on the success of their plans for the capture of Christ; and, as the curtain falls, the cry is raised on every side, "To death with him, to death with him, the enemy of our fathers."

ACT VII.

THE AGONY IN THE GARDEN.

Tableau I. Adam toiling for his Bread in the Sweat of his Brow.—*Gen.* iii. 17–19. This picture is intended to shadow forth the agony of our Lord on the Mount of Olives. As Adam was condemned, in punishment for sin, to eat his bread in the sweat of his face, so, too, in punishment for sin, the Redeemer was covered with a sweat of blood in the Garden of Gethsemani. When the curtain rises Adam, clothed in sheepskins, is seen laboriously tilling the earth. In one hand he holds a spade; with the other he wipes the sweat from his forehead. Eve sits mournfully by with a baby in her arms. Two of her children, in the background, are tearing up thorns and thistles; two others, of more tender years, are playing with a lamb; and one holds an apple in its hand. The Chorus interprets the type and points the moral of the scene.

Tableau II. Joab, on pretence of embracing Amasa, plunges a Sword into his Body.—2 *Kings*, xx. 8–10. Joab, captain of the host of David, is seen near the rock of Gabaon, greeting Amasa with a kiss, while at the same time he basely murders him; a striking type of Judas, who, by a kiss, delivers up Christ into the hands of his enemies. This Tableau gives occasion to a highly poetical address to the rocks of Gabaon.

When the choral chant is ended the garden of Gethsemani is disclosed to view on the inner stage. From behind the scenes Christ advances with his Apostles, and the Agony begins. Leaving the rest of his Apostles behind, he takes with him Peter, James, and John, and he says to them, "My soul is sorrowful even unto death: stay you here and watch with me." Then, going to a little distance, he prays, "Father, thou canst do all things: if it be possible let this chalice pass from me. Nevertheless not my will be done, but thine." Three times he repeats this prayer, and three times he falls to the earth, worn out with suffering and fatigue. In the depth of his bitter agony an Angel comes from Heaven to comfort him. But when, at length, he rises from the earth, drops of blood stand out upon his face, and trickle down upon his purple robe. All this time his chosen Apostles sleep, and when awakened they sleep again.

But Judas, who sleeps not, comes now with a crowd of soldiers and attendants, and saluting his Divine Master, betrays him with a kiss. The soldiers are seized with a sudden awe : at the sound of the Saviour's voice they start back, and fall prostrate to the ground. Peter, with characteristic impetuosity, draws his sword and cuts off the ear of Malchus. For this he is reproved by Christ, and the wounded man is made whole. Then the soldiers, gathering courage from the gentle words and looks of the Saviour, surround him, bind his hands behind his back, and lead him off captive to the city. The terrified Apostles fly in all directions : but, after a little, Peter and John cautiously venture back, and follow the procession at a distance.

This scene, in which the figure and face of Joseph Mair presented, in a surprising degree, that air of serene majesty and patient resignation which has been already noticed, brought home to every mind the utter loneliness and desolation of our Lord in the Garden of Olives. The vast audience was deeply and sensibly affected. None could behold without emotion that sad, pale face bedewed with blood, and that stately form bowed down to the earth from intensity of suffering. For a few minutes the time and place were forgotten; the theatre and the stage disappeared from view; and the sad reality itself was alone present to the mind, and pictured on the imagination.

At this point an interval of an hour was allowed for rest and refreshment. It was a quarter to twelve o'clock: and the Play had gone on continuously for nearly four hours, without the slightest hesitation or failure on the part of the performers, without any symptom of lassitude or inattention on the part of the audience. A change of scene was welcome to every one, and a release from the hard benches of the theatre. In a few minutes the streets of the village were filled with busy groups of men and women; greetings were hurriedly exchanged; and many availed themselves of the opportunity to snatch a hasty repast.

ACT VIII.

CHRIST BEFORE ANNAS.

At half-past twelve the great multitude was again pouring into the theatre, and before the hour had expired, all were in their places, as eager and attentive, under the fierce glare of the meridian sun, as they had been, six hours before, when his first joyous rays shone out above the hills on the east. We had not long to wait. In a few minutes the boom of a gun announced that the second division of the Play was about to begin; and, while its echoes still lingered among the mountains, the Chorus advanced from either side, and sang a plaintive ode, bringing back to our recollection the last sad scene of Gethsemani.

TABLEAU. MICHEAS, THE PROPHET, STRUCK ON THE CHEEK FOR SPEAKING THE TRUTH BEFORE KING ACHAB.— 3 *Kings*, xxii. 10–24. The curtain rises, and a Royal Court is disclosed to view. Achab and Josaphat are seated on thrones and clothed in royal apparel. Before them is a crowd of courtiers and false prophets. The chief of these, Sedecias, is seen in the act of smiting on the cheek Micheas, a prophet of the Lord, because he had ventured to speak unwelcome truth. This picture foreshadows the coming scene in which the Saviour is smitten on the cheek before the tribunal of Annas.

As the curtain falls, shouts are heard in the distance. Annas appears on the balcony of his house, impatiently looking out for his expected victim. Judas enters hurriedly, with a guilty and unquiet air; he pauses before the house of Annas: looks up for a moment, and hears from the old man words of commendation, which must have fallen on his heart as the sentence of his doom, "Thy name shall stand for endless ages at the head of our annals."

Judas passes on, and the shouts of the populace are heard nearer and more violent. Presently, Christ is dragged in by a band of soldiers, surrounded by an infuriated rabble. He is at once conducted into the house of Annas, and immediately after appears on the balcony, in the presence of his judge. His bearing is calm and dignified as before : his face still wears the same expression of patient endurance.

The crowd from below make their accusations against him with great uproar and violence. His enemies are determined not to be satisfied : when he is silent he is blamed for not answering ; when he answers, he is struck on the cheek by a time-serving attendant. In the end, Annas, worn out by his patience, resolves to send him to Caiphas. As he is led away by the soldiers, Peter and John are seen in the distance, still timidly following their Master.

ACT IX.

CHRIST BEFORE CAIPHAS.

TABLEAU I. NABOTH STONED TO DEATH ON THE TESTI-MONY OF FALSE WITNESSES.—3 *Kings*, xxi. 8–13. The innocent Naboth is here represented as a figure of our Lord before Caiphas. For, like Him, he was wrongfully accused of blasphemy, and like Him, too, he was condemned on the evidence of hired witnesses. He is seen on his knees, in the middle of the stage. Round about him the people stand in various attitudes: one, with his arm uplifted, is in the act of throwing a great stone at the innocent victim's head; another is picking up a stone from the ground; others are preparing to lend their aid; others are looking on with approval.

TABLEAU II. THE SUFFERINGS AND PATIENCE OF JOB.—Job is seated on a dunghill, the living picture of human misery and of patient submission. His friends are close by, deriding him for his misfortunes; even his wife is scoffing at him, and seems, with parted lips, on the point of telling him to "Bless God and die."

Christ is now arraigned before Caiphas, who is seen enthroned in the hall of his palace, surrounded by the Chief Priests and the Elders of the people, with the Scribes in attendance. Witness after

witness comes forward to give evidence against him.
But they contradict one another, and seem to agree
only in declaring, at the end, with great vehemence,
"He has blasphemed God, he has deserved death."
At length Caiphas adjures him in the name of the
Living God to say who and what he is. The
Saviour answers with serene dignity, "I am Christ
the Son of God." Then the High Priest rends his
garments, and exclaims, with ill-suppressed delight,
"What need have we of any further witnesses?
You yourselves have heard the blasphemy. What
think ye?" One of the Scribes is then called forth,
who reads, from a great scroll of parchment, the law
concerning the punishment of blasphemy: and all
the members of the Council cry out, with one accord,
"He is guilty of death."

As soon as the judgment is passed the Redeemer
is led away, and, by a change of scene, the outer
court of the palace is before us. Two maids have
kindled a fire, and some of the soldiers are gathered

round it, warming themselves, and talking over the events of the night. Peter and John come timidly from without towards the entrance of the court. John goes in first, and, after a short conference with one of the servants, comes back and brings in Peter. The soldiers make room, and Peter, with a stealthy and suspicious air, takes his place at the fire, which is now burning feebly, and tries to warm himself.

While he is leaning over it one of the maidservants comes up behind, and scrutinizes him all over, with a look of something more than curiosity. She goes round a little to get a better view ; she whispers for a moment to her companion ; they exchange significant glances ; and, at last, she comes up and asks him pertly if *he,* too, was not with Jesus of Galilee. This little bit of acting may be noticed as an example of the conscientious care expended even on the most minute parts of the Passion Play. The maid-servant who identifies Peter appears but a few minutes before the audience : she has but a few words to say. And, yet, her part is performed with as much dramatic skill as if the success òf the Play depended on it alone.

After the third denial of Peter the cock crows. At the same moment Christ is led out from the inner hall, bound iu fetters. He casts a look of mild reproach on Peter, who remembers his Master's warning, and turns away from his glance, full of shame and sorrow. Just before the scene is brought to a close Judas, tortured by a guilty conscience, comes to the house of Caiphas, to find out how the dreadful affair that he has set in motion is going to end. When he sees his Master in bonds, the mockery and the sport of the Roman soldiers, he is filled with remorse, and is heard muttering to himself, as the curtain falls, "Accursed be the deed I have done."

ACT X.

DESPAIR OF JUDAS.

TABLEAU. ABEL KILLED BY HIS BROTHER CAIN.—*Gen.* iv.
3–16. In the middle foreground Cain, with a club in his
hand, is standing, conscience-stricken, over the dead body
of his murdered brother. The Chorus deplores the crime
of the murderer, and depicts the tortures of his guilty
conscience. Restless and unhappy he flies from place to
place; but he cannot fly from himself. Within his soul
the image of his sin is always present as in a mirror; and
it is the contemplation of this image that constitutes his
ever-enduring anguish. So it is now with Judas,

> " Who rushes wildly here and there,
> Until at last, in wild despair,
> He flings away the life that he no more can bear."

What has been foreshadowed in the Tableau, and
portrayed in graphic language by the Chorus, is now
presented to the audience in its vivid reality. On
the inner stage the High Court of the Jews is
sitting once again in council, confirming the sentence
of death pronounced on our Lord by Caiphas.
Judas, in an agony of remorse, rushes into the midst

of the hall, and wants to have the judgment revoked. His vehement expostulations are received with cold indifference by Caiphas and the Priests. When he exclaims, " I have sinned in that I have betrayed innocent blood," they scornfully ask him, " What is that to us ?" adding, that he has had his reward, and that his guilty conscience is his own affair. The miserable man, no longer able to bear the thought of his crime, seizes the money-bag which hangs at his side, flings it violently on the floor at the feet of the High Priest, and rushes headlong from the hall.

Immediately on his departure the money is picked up, and the Chief Priests, in a very business-like fashion, take counsel together how they best may turn it to account. Being the price of blood it cannot be put into the public treasury :-so, after some discussion, they agree to buy with it the potter's field, as a place of burial for strangers. Then, in order to secure the execution of the sentence they

have passed against Christ, they depute three of
their members to seek an audience with the Roman
Governor. These religious men, strict observers of
the law, will not go into Pilate's house, lest they
should become unclean, but ask for an audience
in the garden. The door-keeper listens to their
sanctimonious cant with a knowing leer, and, as
he withdraws to bear their message to his master,
mutters something about the blind hypocrisy of men
" who strain at a gnat and swallow a camel."

A change of scene now brings us to the open
country. Judas is there alone. He cannot venture to approach his Divine Master again ; he has
been ignominiously spurned by the Chief Priests ;
he has no friend to comfort him ; he is alone with
his guilty conscience, the very picture of despair.
As he wanders restlessly about, his wild ravings
fall distinctly on the ear, in the perfect stillness
that now prevails throughout the audience, and
bring out with great force the significance of the

Gospel declaration, that Satan had entered into his soul. Again and again he groans under the torture he is suffering, and repeats the words, "For me there is no hope, no pardon, no redemption." A tree in the distance attracts his notice; he comes nearer to it; glances uneasily upwards; pauses for a moment, as if to reflect; then, in an agony that pierces the heart, exclaims, "I can no longer endure this anguish;" and, as the curtain falls, he is seen in the act of loosening his girdle to make the fatal noose.

ACT XI.

CHRIST AT THE JUDGMENT SEAT OF PILATE.

TABLEAU. DANIEL CONDEMNED TO BE CAST INTO THE DEN OF LIONS.—*Dan.* xiv. 27–30. The King of Babylon is on his throne. Around are the heathen priests, who accuse Daniel of impiety towards the gods, and demand that sentence of death be passed. The king, who, at first, had sought to save him from their malice, yields to their wishes when they threaten to destroy himself and his house. He

JEWISH DIGNITARIES.

SADOC.   NICODEMUS.
AMIEL.   A PHARISEE.

is seen in the act of handing over Daniel to be cast into
the lions' den. This picture is set forth as a figure of
Christ before the tribunal of Pilate. He is accused of
blasphemy by the Jewish Priests, who call for the sentence
of death. Pilate, for a time, resists their clamorous
demands; and would save Christ, if he could do it without
loss to himself. But, when he hears the threat, "If thou
settest this man free thou art not Cæsar's friend," he
yields, and delivers up Christ to be crucified. The Chorus,
as usual, explains the figure, and adds a moral.

  " O Neid! satanisches Gezücht;
   Was unternimmst, was wagst du nicht,
    Um deinen Groll zu stillen?
   Nichts ist dir heilig, nichts zu gut;
   Du opferst Alles deiner Wuth
    Und deinem bösen Willen.

  " Weh dem, den diese Leidenschaft
   In Schlangenketten mit sich rafft!
    Vor neidischen Gelüsten,
   O Brüder! bleibet auf der Hut;
   Nie lasset diese Natternbrut
    In euren Busen nisten."

  " Oh Envy! born of Hell's own brood,
   To feed thy hate, thy thirst of blood,
    What wilt thou not essay!
   Nought will thy rage and malice spare,
   Nought is so holy, nought so fair,
    But it must be thy prey.

" Ah, woe to them and bitter curse,
   Who in their breast this serpent nurse,
      His chains around them binding;
 O brethren, guard your souls with care,
   Let not base Envy enter there,
      Room in your bosoms finding."*

A procession is seen advancing down the streets
of Jerusalem. As it comes near we recognise the
Saviour in fetters, conducted by a band of soldiers, and followed by a motley crowd of people.
Conspicuous in the crowd are the Chief Priests,
the Scribes, and the money-changers. Pilate
comes out, with his attendants, on the balcony of
his house, and looks down with an air of haughty
indifference, almost approaching contempt, on the
surging multitude below. A conference ensues,
in which the calm dignity of the Roman Governor
is brought out in striking contrast with the wrath
and fury of the Jews. The Chief Priests recite
the list of their accusations, "We found this man

* See the Monthly Packet, August, 1871.

perverting our nation; forbidding to give tribute
to Cæsar; calling himself a king." Pilate turns
to Christ and says, "Hast thou nothing to answer to these charges? You see in how many
things they accuse thee." But the Saviour is
silent; and Pilate, wondering at his silence, and
struck by the majesty of his deportment, desires
an audience with him in the judgment hall. The
audience over, he comes out again on the balcony,
and declares that he finds "no guilt in this man."
This announcement is received with fierce cla-
mour by the people. A tumultuous scene ensues.
The Chief Priests repeat their charges, saying, "He
stirreth up the people, teaching throughout all
Judæa, beginning from Galilee, even to this place."
When Pilate hears of Galilee, he asks if "this
man is a Galilean?" and being told that it is so,
he sends him to Herod, the Governor of Galilee,
who has come up to Jerusalem for the Feast of
the Passover.

ACT XII.

CHRIST AT THE COURT OF HEROD.

TABLEAU. SAMSON IN THE HOUSE OF DAGON, THE SPORT
OF THE PHILISTINES.—*Judges*, xvi. 23–30. Samson, the
deliverer of his people, having fallen into the hands of his
enemies, is brought up, in their midst, at a great feast in
the house of Dagon, an object of mockery and derision.
He is seen in the act of grasping the pillars which support
the house, and pulling down the building on the princes
of the Philistines; thus obtaining a triumph in the moment
of his death. So, too, as the Chorus explains, Christ is
derided at the Court of Herod, and, like Samson, by his
death, he triumphs over his enemies.

Herod is seated on his throne, and is evidently
much pleased when the Saviour is brought before
him; for he has heard a great deal of the won-
ders wrought by Jesus of Nazareth. He asks him
many curious questions; but the Son of man is
silent. He calls on him to work a miracle; but
in vain. Then, as if to save his kingly dignity,
which has been thus humbled in the sight of his
courtiers, he delivers him up to the mockery of

the soldiers. They clothe him in a purple garment; they put into his hand a reed for a sceptre; and they hail him, with derisive laughter, as a King. Meanwhile the multitude cry aloud with savage fury, "To death with him, to death with him!" But Herod can find in his conduct nothing deserving of death, and sends him back again to Pilate.

ACT XIII.

JESUS IS SCOURGED AND CROWNED WITH THORNS.

TABLEAU I. JACOB LAMENTING OVER THE BLOOD-STAINED GARMENT OF JOSEPH.—*Gen.* xxxvii. 31–35. This Tableau brings us back again upon the history of Joseph, whom we have already seen sold to the Ismaelite merchants for twenty pieces of silver. His brethren now appear in the presence of their aged father, presenting to him the many-coloured coat of his favourite son, stained with blood. Jacob stands in the background, in an agony of grief; while the Chorus sings a lamentation, and discovers, in the blood-stained coat of Joseph, an image of the Redeemer bleeding from many wounds under the lash of the Roman soldiers.

TABLEAU II. ABRAHAM, ON MOUNT MORIA, SEES A RAM
WITH ITS HEAD ENTANGLED IN THORNS.—*Gen.* xxii. 9–13.
This picture is a symbol of Christ crowned with thorns,
who is chosen by God as a sacrifice for sin, in the place of
mankind, already under sentence of eternal death. Isaac,
his hands bound behind his back, is laid out on the altar
for sacrifice; whilst Abraham, with an expression of
mournful resolution, already holds the knife in his uplifted hand. An angel checks his arm, and points to a
ram with its head entangled in a thorn bush.

It must be admitted that, at this part of the
Play, the Tableaux Vivants, considered as types
of the Passion, are rather fanciful, and sometimes
almost puerile. But this is a defect much more
striking in the description than in the actual representation. These pictures are very useful to
relieve, at intervals, the feelings of the audience,
which, in the more tragic scenes, are often strained
to an almost painful degree of tension. Besides,
however fanciful they may be thought as types,
they are, with few exceptions, beautiful as pictures,
from the artistic grouping of the figures; and are

made still more attractive by the graceful music of the Orchestra and the religious chant of the Chorus. There is much reason to fear that, in the description, they may be found dull, if not wearisome; but all who have seen them will agree that they help very much to embellish the Play.

As the curtain falls on the second Tableau the shouts of the people are heard behind the scenes, "To death with him! To death with him!" · Immediately after, Christ is led in, and brought up before the house of Pilate, who again appears on the balcony. A long and stormy scene ensues, in which the Roman Governor is divided between his sense of justice and his fear of losing favour with the multitude. At length, in the foolish hope of ending the matter by a compromise, he gives Jesus up to be scourged; and the Saviour is led away amidst the shouts of the multitude still calling for his death.

In a few minutes the sound of the lash is heard

behind the curtain of the inner stage : and, as the drop-scene slowly rises, the figure of the Redeemer is seen bound to a pillar, with blood trickling down from his many wounds. The scourging being finished, he is released from the pillar : the purple cloak is again thrown over his shoulders ; the reed is put into his hand ; and he is derided as a mock King. One thing only is wanting, a crown. So the soldiers make a circlet of sharp thorns, and press it down upon his head with two crossed sticks, causing the blood to spurt out over his face. Throughout this scene the roughness and insensibility of the Roman soldiers are faithfully represented. But this only tends to make the effect more impressive, and not less devotional. The spectators learn to feel, as they never felt before, how great was the humiliation of the Saviour of the world : while, at the same time, such is the majesty and unassumed dignity of the suffering Christ, that his divine character is never for a moment forgotten.

ACT XIV.

CHRIST CONDEMNED TO DEATH.

TABLEAU I. JOSEPH HONOURED AS THE FATHER OF HIS
PEOPLE.—*Gen.* xli. 41–43. Seated on a triumphal car,
and clad in silken robes, with a chain of gold about his
neck, Joseph is surrounded by a countless multitude of
people, who hail him with shouts of joy as the saviour
of his country. So, too, the Saviour of the world will soon
be presented to his people: to be received, however, not
like Joseph, with shouts of joy, but with shouts of hatred
and derision.

TABLEAU II. THE SCAPEGOAT SET FREE TO WANDER IN
THE WILDERNESS.—*Levit.* xvi. 7–10. Moses is kneeling
before the altar. The goat that has been slain by Aaron
for the sins of the people lies bleeding on one side: while
the emissary goat is on the point of being dismissed, to
wander free in the desert. In like manner, as the Chorus
sings, interpreting the type, Barabbas is set free, and
Christ is offered in sacrifice for the sins of mankind. The
chant of the Chorus is, at intervals, interrupted by the
cries of the populace behind the scenes; and a fine effect
is produced, which may vie with the greatest triumphs of
dramatic skill. The German text of this passage has been
turned into English by a distinguished writer, who brings
out, with great felicity, the spirit as well as the sense of
the original words.

CHOR. " Ich höre schon ein Mordgeschrei :"

VOLK. " Barabbas sei
" Von Banden frei !"

CHOR. " Nein, Jesus sei
" Von Banden frei !—
" Wild tönet, ach ! der Mörder Stimm' :"

VOLK. " Ans Kreuz mit ihm ! ans Kreuz mit ihm !"

CHOR. " Ach, seht ihn an ! ach, seht ihn an !
" Was hat er Böses denn gethan ?"

VOLK. " Entlässest du den Büsewicht,
" Dann bist des Kaisers Freund du nicht."

CHOR. " Jerusalem ! Jerusalem !
" Das Blut des Sohnes rächet noch an euch der Herr !"

VOLK. " Es falle über uns und unsre Kinder her !"

CHOR. " Es komme über euch und eure Kinder !"

CHORUS. " I hear approach a murderous cry :"

PEOPLE. " Let Barabbas be
" From his bonds set free !"

CHORUS. " Nay, let Jesus be
" From his bonds set free !
" Wildly sounds the murderers' cry."

PEOPLE. " Crucify him ! crucify !"

CHORUS. " Ah, look on him ! Behold the Man !
 " Oh, say what evil hath he done !"

PEOPLE. " If thou settest this man free,
 " Cæsar's friend thou canst not be."

CHORUS. " Jerusalem ! Jerusalem ! Woe, woe to thee !
 " The blood of Christ by God avenged shall be !"

PEOPLE. " His blood on us and on our children fall !"

CHORUS. " Yea, upon you, and on your children all !"*

The shouts of the people come nearer and nearer
as the Choristers retire ; and soon the stage is filled
with an angry and excited multitude, clamouring,
before the house of Pilate, for the death of Christ.
Pilate appears on the balcony, and with him appears
the Saviour, clad in his purple robe, with the reed
in his hand, and the crown of thorns on his head.
Some hope still lingers in the breast of the Roman
Governor that he may move the multitude to
compassion ; and pointing to the suffering, but still

* See Macmillan's Magazine, October, 1860.

majestic, form of the Redeemer, he presents him to the people with the well-known words, " Behold the Man." But he only provokes the fury of the rabble, who cry aloud with ever increasing violence, "To death with him! To death with him! Crucify him! Crucify him!"

One expedient yet remains. Even a condemned criminal may be released by the people on occasion of the great festival that is now at hand. Surely this clemency may be exercised in favour of Christ. To make the appeal more effective, Barabbas, an outcast of society, is brought up from his prison cell, and set before the people. Poor old Johann Allinger, who represents this character, manages to assume the look and bearing of a low-bred ruffian. As he stands beside the Christ, and the people are called upon to make a choice between them, it is impossible not to feel a new sense of the infinite depth of humiliation to which our Lord descended for the sins of men.

The multitude demand to have Barabbas set free

"Ecce Homo." "Mater Dolorosa."

and Christ condemned to death. Pilate hesitates.
A message comes from his wife, warning him to
have no share in this evil work. But the Chief
Priests, who have been busy, all along, among the
people, now come to the front, and, with wicked in-
genuity, remind him that Christ had set himself up
for a King; adding the significant threat, "If thou
settest this man free, thou art not Cæsar's friend."
This is decisive. The refined and courtly Roman,
who loves his own ease and dignity more than he
loves justice, will not risk the Emperor's displeasure
to save an innocent man. Nevertheless he seeks, by
a flimsy sophistry, to clear his soul from the appearance of guilt. He calls for water and a basin; washes
his hands in the presence of the crowd; and then
pronounces sentence of death, declaring, at the same
time, "I am innocent of the blood of this just man:
look you to it." And the exulting shouts of the
multitude rend the air as they cry, "His blood be
upon us and on our children."

ACT XV.

THE JOURNEY TO CALVARY.

TABLEAU I. ISAAC CARRYING THE WOOD FOR THE SACRI-
FICE.—*Gen.* xxii. 6–8. Isaac, devoted to death by God's
command, is seen climbing the hill of Moria by the
side of Abraham, his father, and bearing on his back the
wood for the sacrifice of which he is to be himself the
victim. Thus, too, the Chorus tells us, will Jesus carry
his cross to Calvary.

> " Betet an und habet Dank;
>   Der den Kelch der Leiden trank,
>   Geht nun in den Kreuzestod,
>   Und versöhnt die Welt mit Gott.

> " Wie das Opferholz getragen
>   Isaak selbst auf Moria,
>   Wanket, mit dem Kreuz beladen,
>   Jesus hin nach Golgotha."

> " Adore and bless the Lord; for He
>   Who drank the cup of agony,
>   Treadeth now death's painful road,
>   To reconcile the world with God.

"As Isaac bore the fire and wood
Whereon he must a victim die,
So, laden with the bitter Rood,
Jesus goes to Calvary."*

TABLEAU II. A BRAZEN SERPENT IS RAISED ALOFT BY
MOSES IN THE DESERT.—*Numb.* xxi. 6–9. The Israelites,
encamped in the wilderness of Sin, suffer great torment
from the bites of fiery serpents. Moses, by command of
God, raises on high a brazen serpent; a type of Christ
raised up on the cross for the salvation of men. The
Chorus interprets the type in song.

TABLEAU III. THE ISRAELITES LOOK AT THE BRAZEN SER-
PENT, AND ARE HEALED.—*Numb.* xxi. 6–9. This picture
exhibits again the same group of men, women, and children. In the midst of them is a great wooden cross,
round the arms of which is coiled the brazen serpent.
Moses points to it as the remedy for their sufferings; and
the eyes of all the people are fixed on it. So, too, the
Chorus sings, they who look up to the Redeemer on the
cross will be healed from their sins.

The sound of many voices is now heard from
afar: and, presently, a noisy and excited crowd
is seen filing down the street, on the right hand

---

* See the Monthly Packet, September, 1871.

side of the stage. At the head of the procession
appears the Christ, his pale face bedewed with
drops of blood, and his stately form bowed down
under the weight of a heavy wooden cross.
Around him are the Roman soldiers, men of
stalwart limbs and unfeeling hearts, who urge
him on with stripes when he pauses, for a moment,
from utter weariness and exhaustion. The captain
of the band is on horseback, and bears aloft a
standard, the symbol of Roman authority.

Next come the two thieves, attended by their
executioners, and laden, in like manner, each
with the cross on which he is to suffer. But they
are fresh and vigorous, and swagger on with an
air of careless indifference. Lastly come the Chief
Priests, and Pharisees, and the money changers
of the temple, with a countless multitude of men
and women, old and young.

At length the Saviour totters, and falls to the
ground. The Chief Priests are angry at the

delay; and Simon of Cyrene, who happens to come up at the time, is roughly seized hold of, and compelled to carry the cross. A group of pious women, shortly afterwards, meet the procession with wailing and lamentation. The Redeemer turns to them, with a countenance of love and compassion; and, breaking at last the silence he has kept so long, he says, " Daughters of Jerusalem, weep not for me, but weep for yourselves and your children." The voice is low and weak; but so solemn and distinct is the utterance, so still the audience, that every syllable is · heard throughout the vast assembly, and silent tears flow fast. As the procession advances, Mary, the mother of Christ, attended by Saint John and the pious women, amongst whom it is easy to recognize the Magdalen, approaches towards it from one of the side streets. The mother exchanges glances with her son, and follows in mournful silence. And all move on to Calvary.

ACT XVI.

THE CRUCIFIXION.

As the procession disappears in the distance the Choristers enter, as usual, from each side of the stage. But they have laid aside their brilliant robes, and now appear in garments of deepest mourning. There is no Tableau : but the leader of the Chorus, in a plaintive monologue, calls on the audience to come with hearts full of compassion and gratitude to Calvary, where the Redeemer, " silent, patient, and forgiving," is crucified for the sins of men. As he proceeds, the dull, heavy blows of a hammer are heard behind the curtain of the inner stage : and he describes the scene which, though out of view, is, by those sounds, made vividly present to every imagination.

Passing, at length, almost imperceptibly, from monologue to chant, he sings of Christ's love for man : and then, joined by the whole Chorus, he calls on all present, in return for this love, to bring with them love and devotion to the altar of the Cross.

> " Wer kann die hohe Liebe fassen
>   Die bis zum Tode liebt,
>   Und, statt der Mörder Schaar zu hassen,
>   Noch Segnend ihr vergibt ?

> " O bringet dieser Liebe
>   Nur fromme Herzenstriebe
>   Am Kreuzaltar
>   Zum Opfer dar ! "

> " Who can that tender love conceive
>   Which loveth unto death,
>   Which ev'n its murderers doth forgive,
>   And bless with dying breath ?

> " Oh, then, this love returning,
>   Bring hearts with true love burning,
>   An offering meet
>   To Jesus' feet." *

The Chorus retires : the curtain rises. Two crosses are standing erect, one on either side, to which the

---

* See the Monthly Packet, September, 1871.

two thieves are already bound by strong cords passing round their arms and legs. In the centre of the stage a third cross, on which is seen the figure of the Christ, is stretched along the ground. At a given signal it is raised in the air bearing its victim aloft : with a perceptible jerk it falls into a socket prepared for it ; and the scene of the Crucifixion is before us in living reality.

To all appearance the body of Joseph Mair, which is covered with a tight fitting, flesh coloured garment, and has a cincture of white linen, loosely folded round, at the waist, is fastened to the cross by large rough nails that pierce his hands and feet. The arms are stretched out almost horizontally as in the picture of Guido Reni : the feet are placed one above the other, with a slender support beneath, and are fastened by a single nail ; the head, which still wears its crown of thorns, is slightly bowed down on the breast. Blood oozes from all the wounds, and trickles slowly to the ground.

The Crucifixion.

All the details of the Gospel history are minutely and faithfully reproduced. The excited and turbulent crowd is there, with its blasphemies and shouts of derision. The Chief Priests and the Scribes stand by, full of triumph and scorn. The Roman soldiers, rough and unfeeling, divide among themselves the garments of the Man of Sorrows, and cast lots for his seamless tunic. All this time the three bodies are suspended in the air, and one almost begins to fancy it is a picture or a vision, until at length voices are heard from the crosses on either side, above the storm that rages below. One of the malefactors joins in the blasphemies of the crowd : the other rebukes him, and appeals for mercy to the Saviour suffering by his side. Then the Central Figure, in which the sympathies of all are concentrated, is seen to move its lips, and the well-known words are heard, "Amen I say to thee, this day thou shalt be with me in paradise."

As time wears on, the Virgin Mother, with the

pious women and Saint John, comes close up to
the cross. When Christ sees his mother standing
there, and the disciple that he loves, he says to
his mother, "Woman, behold thy son," and to
the disciple, "Behold thy mother." And so, one
by one, those beautiful sentences fall on the ear,
which once fell from the Redeemer's lips on
Calvary, until, with a great effort, the last words
are pronounced, "It is consummated," and his
head falls down lifeless on his breast.

A loud crash, as if of thunder, is heard behind the
scenes. Presently, a messenger rushes in with the
news that the veil of the Temple is rent in twain
from top to bottom. The Chief Priests start back
in terror and dismay, and, eagerly discoursing among
themselves, withdraw from the scene. Then come the
executioners to examine the bodies. Finding the
thieves still living, they strike them violently with
clubs on the legs and chest until they expire. They
are coming towards the Christ, when Mary Magdalen

rushes forward, and, with outstretched arms, presses them back, exclaiming that they have already done enough. Not much do they care for her interference; but, seeing that the Christ is already dead, they are content. Nevertheless a soldier, coming up with a lance, pierces the left side, and a stream of blood gushes out. The bodies of the malefactors are now quickly uncorded and carried away by the executioners; the crowd gradually disperses; and the Christ, still hanging on the cross, is left to the pious care of his friends.

Joseph of Arimathea, who had sought and obtained the necessary authority from Pilate, proceeds to take down the body and prepare it for sepulture. In this he is assisted by Nicodemus, who has come provided with spices. A ladder is placed in front of the cross and another behind it. Joseph mounts in front, and having first, with great tenderness, removed the crown of thorns, receives from Nicodemus, who is on the ladder behind, a long roll of stout linen cloth. This he places across the chest and under the arms of the body: the ends are then taken up behind the shoulders, and passed over the arms of the cross, so as to fall down behind to the ground. They are received below and held fast by two men, while the nails are slowly, and, as it would seem, with difficulty, extracted. Then the linen cloth is gradually relaxed, and the body, supported in front by Joseph, is gently and reverently lowered to the ground. Here it is received on a large linen sheet, and stretched out at length, with the head reclining on the lap of the Virgin Mother, as we have so often seen represented in pictures and statuary. Nicodemus now applies his spices: the linen cloth is folded round the body: it is carried, with great reverence, to the sepulchre at the back of the stage; and, as they roll up a large stone to close the entrance, the curtain slowly falls.

This long and affecting scene, considered merely from a dramatic point of view, seemed to be as near perfection as human acting well could be; and they who have witnessed it will probably have carried away, in their minds, an image of the Crucifixion which will take the place, as a gifted writer has said, of all the pictures they have ever seen, and all the descriptions they have ever heard. The figure of the Christ hung upon the cross pretty much as we are accustomed to conceive it; but, as I thought, with a beauty of outline such as I had never seen equalled in painting or sculpture. The means by which it is fastened to the cross are, I believe, not exactly known. To the audience there is no support visible but the three nails, and the small rest under the feet. It is, however, generally supposed that the body is mainly suspended by means of a stout strap passing round the waist and attached to the cross behind; that a small elastic band round each wrist helps to support the arms; and that a similar band bears, in part, the weight of the legs. The body hung on the cross exactly eighteen minutes; fifteen from the time that the cross was raised in the air until Nicodemus mounted the ladder, and three more while he was extracting the nails and arranging the linen band by which it was lowered to the ground.

ACT XVII.

THE RESURRECTION.

It has been said more than once by English critics that the Play should end with the scene of the Crucifixion; for, at this point, the interest of the audience has been raised to the highest degree of intensity. If the object of the Play were simply to produce a powerful dramatic effect, this criticism would be perfectly just. But, happily, the pious villagers of Ober-Ammergau never conceived the idea of turning the Passion of our Lord into a sensation drama. It was their high and noble purpose to impress upon common minds, in a vivid and enduring way, the doctrine of the Fall and Redemption of mankind; and this great lesson would have been incomplete if they left out the final triumph of the Redeemer in his Resurrection and glorious Ascension.

TABLEAU I. JONAS SAVED FROM THE DEPTHS OF THE SEA, AND CAST UP ON DRY LAND.—*Jonas*, ii., *Matt.* xii. 39, 40. This Tableau, though not very effective as a picture, presents a type of the Resurrection which was pointed out by our Lord himself. When the Pharisees arrogantly called on him to work a miracle He rebuked them, and said that no sign should be given them but the sign of the prophet Jonas. As Jonas, after three days and three nights in the depths of the sea, was delivered safe on dry land by the power of God, so, on the third day after his death, would the Son of Man be delivered from the · grave. In the background is the troubled sea, with a

ship sailing away in the distance. Nearer is seen the
whale, with its vast jaws widely distended ; and Jonas
is just stepping from the waters on dry land. The
Choristers, who have resumed their bright robes of many
colours, explain the type in song.

TABLEAU II. THE PASSAGE OF THE RED SEA.—*Exod.* xiv.
13–31. In the foreground stand Moses and the children
of Israel, who have passed in safety. Further off, Pharao
and his hosts are seen struggling with the waves. So,
too, the Chorus sings, does Christ come forth triumphant
from the grave, and so, too, are his enemies overthrown.

Four soldiers are holding guard round the
sepulchre in which the Christ was laid. An
Angel appears, shining brightly, and rolls away
the great stone from the entrance : the rumbling
noise of an earthquake is heard ; and Christ,
encompassed with light, comes forth from the
tomb, passes through the group, and quickly disappears. The soldiers, terrified by the noise and
dazzled by the light, fall prostrate to the ground,
as dead men. After a little they recover, and
hurry off to bring the news into the city. Mary
Magdalen and the pious women come to the

sepulchre, with spices and precious ointments. Finding the tomb empty, they are filled with consternation. But an Angel consoles them, announcing the joyful tidings: "Fear not; for I know that you seek Jesus who was crucified. He is not here, for He is risen as He said. Come and see the place where the Lord was laid. And go quickly, and tell his disciples that He is risen from the dead: and behold He will go before you into Galilee; there you shall see Him." And they went forth quickly with great joy to tell the disciples.

Then the Chief Priests come back with the soldiers, and seeing that, in truth, the stone was rolled away and the body gone, they offer them money, saying, "You must say his disciples came at night and stole the body while you were asleep." The soldiers agree and take the money, all but one, who stoutly holds out and protests, "By my honour, I'll tell everything just as it occurred." Next come Peter and John, who look into the tomb and go away. Lastly, Mary Magdalen comes again; and to her the Christ appears. At first she takes Him for the gardener, and scarcely looks at Him: her eyes are fixed on the empty sepulchre. But when she hears from His lips the single word "Maria," she turns quickly round, glances up for a moment, and sinks down at His feet.

———

CLOSING HYMN OF TRIUMPH.

WITH ALLEGORICAL TABLEAU OF THE ASCENSION.

The Choristers enter for the last time and sing, in joyous strains, a chant of praise and triumph.

> " Ueberwunden, überwunden
> Hat der Held der Feinde Macht:
> Er, Er schlummerte nur Stunden
> In der düstern Grabesnacht.

" Singet Ihm in heil'gen Psalmen;
 Streuet Ihm des Sieges Palmen;
  Auferstanden ist der Herr!
 Jauchzet Ihm ihr Himmel zu!
 Sing' dem Sieger, Erde, du!
  Halleluja Dir Erstandner!

" Preis Ihm, dem Todesüberwinder,
  Der einst verdammt auf Gabbatha!
 Preis Ihm, dem Heiliger der Sünder,
  Der für uns starb auf Golgotha!"

" Conquering and to conquer all
  Forth He comes in all His might;
 Slumbering but a few short hours
  In the grave's funereal night.

" Sing to him in holy psalms!
 Strew before Him victory's palms!
  Christ the Lord of life is risen!
 Sound, O heavens, with anthems meet;
 Earth, with songs the conqueror greet!
  Hallelujah! Christ is risen!

" Praise be to Him who conquers death,
  Who once was judged on Gabbatha!
 Praise be to Him who heals our sins,
  Who died for us on Golgotha!"*

---

* See Macmillan's Magazine, October, 1860.

The curtain rises, and a brilliant scene is before us. High in the centre of the background is the Christ encompassed with a halo of light. His glorified face is turned towards Heaven, to which he is about to ascend. His right hand is raised as if to bless : in his left he carries the banner of victory. The wounds in his hands, his feet, and his left side, are distinctly visible, and shine with a peculiar radiance. Close to him stand his blessed mother and his Apostles : while around are grouped the saints of the Old Covenant; the Patriarchs and Prophets, Moses with the Tables of the Law, and David with his harp. At a little distance, on lower ground, are his enemies humbled and prostrate; the Chief Priests and the money-changers, Pilate and Herod, the soldiers and the rabble.

All the various figures are motionless except the Saviour, who slowly rises in the air, still looking up to Heaven : and the curtain only

THE ENEMIES OF CHRIST.

PILATE.	ROMAN CAPTAIN.
CAIPHAS.	HEROD.

falls when he seems on the point of passing out of view. Meanwhile the hymn of triumph proceeds.

"Bringt Lob und Preis dem Höchsten dar,
Dem Lamme das getödtet war!
Halleluja!
Das Siegreich aus dem Grab hervor
Sich hebet im Triumph empor!
Halleluja! Halleluja!

"Ja lasst des Bundes Harfe klingen,
Dass Freude durch die Seele bebt!
Lasst uns dem Sieger Kronen bringen,
Der auferstand und ewig lebt.

"Lobsinget alle Himmelsheere!
Dem Herrn sei Ruhm und Herrlichkeit!
Anbetung, Macht, und Kraft, und Ehre,
Von Ewigkeit zu Ewigkeit!"

"Praise Him who now on high doth reign!
Praise to the Lamb that once was slain!
Hallelujah!
Praise Him who, glorious from the grave,
Comes forth triumphantly to save!
Hallelujah!

" Let Israel's harp with gladdening sound
    Joy through every spirit pour ;
He with the conqueror's crown is crowned,
    Who died, and lives for evermore.

" O praise Him, all ye hosts of Heaven !
    To Him all praise and glory be !
To Him be adoration given,
    Through ages of eternity !"

And so, at a quarter to five in the afternoon,
when the summer sun was already sinking to the
west, ended the Passion Play, which had begun
at eight in the morning. The feelings of the
audience, for so many hours carefully suppressed,
broke forth in a loud murmur of admiration. But
there was no clapping of hands, no noisy applause ; for every one seemed instinctively to feel
that such demonstrations, however natural and
well-deserved, would be at once unsuited to the
sacred character of the Play, and unwelcome to
the high spirit and the religious earnestness of the
performers. The great multitude, as if under the

influence of some potent charm, quietly broke up and melted away. A few groups only lingered behind; and, with a sort of awe mingled with curiosity, watched the village actors as they emerged from the rere of the Theatre, and modestly wended their way to their rustic homes.

I have endeavoured, in the foregoing pages, to give, with very little comment of my own, a plain account of what I saw and heard at the Passion Play; believing that my readers would much prefer to learn exactly what it was, than to hear what I thought about it. But now that my task is nearly done, it will not be out of place to record the effect produced on those who were present, and the impression carried away when the Play was over. Nothing is more remarkable than the unanimity with which men of every variety of character, and of widely different positions in society, have expressed themselves on this subject. With very few exceptions, they all agree in saying that the Passion Play at Ober-Ammergau, as a religious spectacle, is instructive and edifying, while, from an artistic point of view, it is a drama of great power and absorbing interest.

Here are a few sentences hastily gathered, almost at random, from writers who, to say the least, are free from every suspicion of undue prepossession in favour of the Play :—

The *Times'* Correspondent writes : "I have never seen so affecting a spectacle, or one more calculated to draw out the best and purest feelings of the heart. It is, of course, impossible to answer for the feelings of others ; but I can say for myself, and for several spectators of the Play whom I have consulted, that there was nothing from the beginning to the end that need shock the most sensitive religious instinct." *

An article in *Macmillan's Magazine,* which is commonly ascribed to an eminent Divine of high position in the Church of England, bears witness that from this Play the "German peasants carry away, graven on their memories, the chief facts and doctrines both of the Old and New Testament, with an exactness such as would be vainly sought in the masses of our poorer population, or even, it may be said, with some of our clergy." †

An Englishwoman, writing home, says : "The simple grandeur of the Christ was almost awful. I forgot all but the wonderful story of our salvation, and cried all day." ‡

"The effect upon all who were present," says a

---

* The Ober-Ammergau Passion Play ; reprinted from the *Times:* by the Rev. Malcolm M'Coll, M.A., pp. 84, 85.

† Macmillan's Magazine, October, 1860, p. 447.

‡ Quoted by Mr. Blackburn, Art in the Mountains, p. 143.

writer for the *Graphic*, "was solemn to an extraordinary degree; there was nothing to shock the most sensitive religious instincts, and little for the most critical to disapprove of." *

From the same writer we have the following: "There was one figure sitting near us during the day,—a well-known face, and a well known name in London society,—whose customary place at that hour in the afternoon was the bow window of a west-end club, who was literally bathed in tears." †

An Oxonian gives a striking account of the struggle in his mind between the influence of prejudice and the influence of the Play: "All through the Play I kept repeating to myself, 'This is a primitive, mediæval, half-civilised peasantry, still sunk in the trammels of priestcraft; it has never known what it is to have an open

---

* Art in the Mountains; by Henry Blackburn; p. 141.
† Ibid, p. 143.

Bible and a free press; it is deprived of the bless-
ings of the electric telegraph, and is about three
hundred years behind the present age.' But it
would not do. I could not but confess that I was
witnessing not only a beautiful, but a most subtle,
and delicate, and thoughtful rendering of the
Gospel history."*

Even the *Saturday Review* forgets its wonted
asperity, and speaks with kindness of the Passion
Play, which it regards as "a means of decided
moral and intellectual improvement." †

And a favourite novelist, the author of *Quits*,
tells us that her heroine felt that the Play "would
take the place of all the pictures and statues she
had ever seen, and remain indelibly impressed on
her mind for ever."‡

---

* Impressions of the Ober-Ammergau Passion Play, by an Oxonian,
p. 25.

† Saturday Review, September 24, 1871.

‡ Quits, by the Baroness Tautphœus, vol. i., chap. xviii.

To these interesting testimonies I may, perhaps, be allowed to add the evidence of my own
experience.   I went to Ober-Ammergau with a
prejudice against the Passion Play.   It seemed to
me, though I could not exactly tell why, that a
certain irreverence was involved in the very idea
of such a representation.   And, moreover, I
greatly feared that, from want of skill on the part
of village actors, events the most sacred in the
eyes of all Christians would be brought into un-
pleasant contact with grotesque and ludicrous
associations.   But no sooner had the Play com-
menced than my prejudices were dispelled.   It
became at once manifest that a spirit of deep religious reverence pervaded the performance; and
that with this was combined a degree of artistic
taste which could not fail to win the respect and
admiration of every cultivated mind.   I was more
sensibly impressed than ever I had been by any
sermon, however eloquent: and, when I left the

theatre, I felt that the history of our Lord's Passion had been stamped on my mind in a series of vivid pictures which could not easily be effaced.

Nevertheless, I am no advocate for the more frequent repetition of the Passion Play, nor for its extension beyond the village of Ober-Ammergau. The peculiar combination of circumstances which, in the course of many generations, has brought it to its present perfection in this mountain hamlet, could not, I think, be found elsewhere in the world; nor could they long subsist, even here, without the protection which is afforded by its rare recurrence. The curiosity of visitors would easily degenerate into irreverence, and the simple piety of the people would inevitably suffer from frequent contact with an ever-changing concourse of tourists. The most that I can venture to hope is, that the Passion Play at Ober-Ammergau may long continue to be surrounded by the safeguards which have hitherto protected its religious character; and that, as each ten years come round, it may still be repeated in the same earnest spirit of devotion, and with the same artistic taste, from which so many thousands have drawn edification and instruction in the summer of 1871.

THE END.

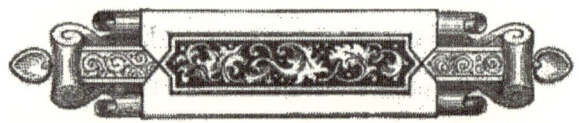

LITERARY NOTICES.

—:o:—

Church Opinion.—January 13, 1872.

" We know of no work which gives so graphic, complete, and able an account of the Passion Play, as the one before us by Doctor Molloy. The introductory part, which describes the origin and history of the Play, its scope and design, the place, the people, and the theatre, is delightfully simple, and gives the reader a most vivid picture of the circumstances under which the drama was produced. Some excellent photographic views illustrate the scenes and characters described, and aid in producing so tasteful a volume, that, considering its literary merits as well, we cannot do otherwise than recommend it most heartily to all our readers "

Dublin Evening Mail.—December 11, 1871.

" Doctor Molloy's book will well repay every reader, and ought, in fact, to find a place in every library, as at once a very suggestive and a very beautiful account of one of the most striking features of religious enthusiasm these later centuries have seen."

The Irish Times.— December 26, 1871.

" Doctor Molloy's language is classical in its simplicity, elegance, and force, and his description of the various parts of the Play gives a vivid and impressive picture of this singular and suggestive drama. The work is very handsomely brought out, and is certain to command an extensive sale, but not more extensive than it deserves."

The Tablet.—December 30, 1871.

" It has been a happy idea on the part of Dr. Molloy to add photographs to his very interesting description of the Ammergau Passion Play. . . . His account is the only complete one which has yet appeared, and therefore a more valuable, though a more expensive, book than any we have previously reviewed on this subject."

The Freeman's Journal.—December 11, 1871.

" One of the most beautiful books that could be selected for presentation."